About the Author:

Skyler is a 12-year-old with a love of learning, boundless curiosity, and wild imagination. He loves to read, especially what-if scenarios based on historical events. His favorite board game is Axis and Allies. Combining all of these, he wrote his first short novel over winter break this year. This is his first published work.

I have always been interested in World War 2, especially what-if scenarios. It first started when I came up with an idea inspired by the Axis and Allies Zombies broad game, especially the fictional newspapers and reports throughout the rulebook. It wasn't meant to be a massive story, but rather just a short idea improvised. I decided that the concepts, world building, and relationship to Axis and Allies had to be refined, so I wrote a more detailed story. Thank you especially to Mr. Layden for writing the foreword and to Ms. Tina Hugall for being the first one to review my story!

-Skyler Cheung

Foreword:

The term "What if?" is not simply something this author uses in conversation, as it is a jumping off point to his creative process. As a teacher of Social Studies and Language Arts at Tyee Middle School I have known Skyler Cheung as a middle school student for 2 years and in that time have grown to appreciate his creativeness, prowess in the research absorption of immense detail, and his near constant use of the term "What if?". On many an afternoon we have discussed the pivotal battles and scenarios that could have swung World War 2 in vastly different directions. Add to this a creative X factor and what we have is a passion project on World War 2, and an imaginative use of zombie lore, to create a scenario of immense scope to match Skyler's immense knowledge of the battles of World War. As such, a knowledge of these battles is necessary to understand this work, and when one does an appreciation for the freshness of his ideas is certainly a result upon reading. As I sit in my summer bathed living room pondering the new school year, I imagine Skyler is pondering another imaginative scenario to discuss, and a new twist on "What if?". May he never stop researching, writing… and imagining.

By Chris Layden
Teacher, Tyee Middle School

CHAPTER 1: THE ZOMBIES STRIKE! 13

CHAPTER 2: KILLER ZOMBIES 16

CHAPTER 3: THE ZOMBIE'S PACIFIC WAR......................19

CHAPTER 4: TECHNOLOGY AND ZOMBIES......................23

CHAPTER 5: DEATH TO THE ZOMBIES! 29

CHAPTER 6: ZOMBIE HOPPING 32

CHAPTER 7: ZOMBIE BREAKTHROUGH..........................39

CHAPTER 8: THE ZOMBIE'S EUROPEAN WAR 44

CHAPTER 9: ZOMBIE POWER 49

CHAPTER 10: LAND OF THE ZOMBIES............................56

CHAPTER 11: BATTLESHIPS, CRUISERS, AND ZOMBIES ...66

CHAPTER 12: THE LAST ZOMBIE.....................................70

Zombie rules: The infection is spread via smoke reaching dead bodies. However, the dead bodies must be created (which means that the person who was in the body is killed) on the day that the game starts or later. This starts in 1942, although sightings have been seen since at least the Battle of Smolensk.

Chapter 1: The Zombies Strike!

As the Soviet Winter offensive grinds to a halt, the first zombies come out and force the Soviets to garrison many forces there. Due to the zombies killing many Soviet soldiers, more zombies come out, creating a never-ending cycle, consuming large amounts of manpower. The Soviets start developing Z-4 explosives for their artillery. Meanwhile, Hitler, realizing that Romanian oil reserves are running low, decides to launch an offensive south into the Caucasus to capture the vast oil fields there. At this point, increasingly large numbers of zombies are appearing from partisan battles in the rear. The assault is a success, pushing the Soviets back, capturing Rostov. However, zombie attacks force the Axis to station the Italian Eighth Army and Romanian Third Army to defend against these attacks as the German Second and Fourth Panzer Armies and the Hungarian Second Army drive toward Voronezh and the German Sixth Army pushes towards the Volga, near Stalingrad (although the capture of it is not deemed necessary). As the Battle of Voronezh rages, zombies start to interfere in the operations of both sides in the area, becoming a third power in the battle. Meanwhile, as the Sixth Army reaches the Volga with air superiority, the zombie menace grows to an amount that the generals decide to advise Hitler to create a Russian Liberation Army, to acquire badly needed supplies of manpower to combat the zombie threat. Hitler is convinced and approves the plan, as German scientists race to invent the zombie mind control ray. In order to amass as much manpower as possible for the Russian Liberation Army, all prisoners of war are ordered to be treated as well as possible, and all Einsatzgruppen are reformed into Waffen-SS divisions. All German troops will be given an education to make them believe, despite years of linked anti Slavic ant Communist themes, that communism is the true enemy of Germany and Germany must liberate the Soviet people from communism so they can be productive members in European society. Several self-governing regions are created, areas where the native peoples get to manage most aspects of their region. However, all men raised for military operations will be assigned to the Russian Liberation Army.

Chapter 2: Killer Zombies

With both sides exhausted from the Battle of Voronezh and the Volga, the German First Panzer and Seventeenth Armies, along with the Romanian Fourth Army and the elite mountain troops of the Alpini corps of the Italian Eighth Army, advance south into the vast oil fields of Maykop and Baku. German air superiority and transport facilitate the advance, although zombie attacks slow down the advance. Chechen forces, however, help take certain oil fields before they are destroyed by the Soviets, making the attacks by the Axis profitable. However, operations behind the Soviet lines by the Chechens are hampered by Chechen opposition to the Germans hiring the Cossacks, enemies of the Chechens to fight the Soviets. As the great battles on the Eastern Front take place, after the great Battle of Gazala in North Africa, Operation Herkules was launched, with Malta falling, but with casualties on the Axis side high due to strong British resistance and zombie attacks. With supplies easily travelling towards Tobruk, Tripoli, and Benghazi,

Rommel moves eastward into Egypt, driving towards El Alamein, with his advance halted there. As both sides rebuild their forces, Rommel launches an offensive at Alam El Hafa, just as the Americans land in Vichy French North Africa in Operation Torch. Zombie attacks cause havoc for both the Germans and British, with Rommel breaking through just as the Americans captured Algiers. The British, with vast amounts of supplies coming in, were able to hold Alexandria and launch a counteroffensive, pushing Rommel out of Egypt. Zombie attacks slow the British and American advance, allowing Rommel to escape through zombies into western Libya. With zombie attacks preventing the British from destroying Rommel's force, the British and the Americans start developing Z.I.B.R.A suits and chainsaw tanks. As 1942 ends, the Battles of The Rhzev Salient end with a Soviet defeat, and zombies crawling all over the salient. To tie down Soviet forces, Germany withdraws from the salient, redeploying those divisions as well as forces freed up from rear security duty and the Russian Liberation Army's occupation of part of the central sector of the front to strengthen German defenses against the planned Soviet winter offensive. Meanwhile, Rommel's reinforcements, well supplied from Malta, dig in, slowly giving up heavily contested areas, forcing the Allies to fight the many zombies there. The Battle of The Caucasus ends in success, with Axis forces reaching Gronzy and digging in to withstand the Soviet winter counteroffensive and break through into Baku.

Chapter 3: The Zombie's Pacific War

Realizing that Japan cannot fight a two-ocean war, despite heavy American pressure, Japan is able to force Britain to sue for peace. This also helps the British, as it enables them to concentrate all forces against Hitler and the zombie menace. When the Americans landed at Guadalcanal, after launching a fierce counterattack in the Battle of Savo Island destroying many important transports and supply ships in the process, and evacuating Imperial Japanese Army forces stationed on Guadalcanal and the surrounding islands, the IJN fell back to better defensive positions near Rabul. Realizing the need to delay the American advance for as long as possible, the Japanese launch a massive escort program similar to the Allied programs during the time of the Battle of The Atlantic, to make reinforcing defensive positions easier and therefore causing as many casualties as possible in the island battles. This effort is done concurrently with the development of deadnapper convoys, involving the movement of zombies via transports to make up for the shortage of manpower to the Pacific islands from China. After Hitler's bombing of Stalingrad brought the smoke to this area, there were large effects due to the large amounts of infantry fighting on the frontline. The deadnapper convoy system not only lessens the pressure felt by the hard-pressed Japanese troops in China, but also brings large amounts of defenders to less important islands that could be invaded, freeing up regular troops for the defense of Rabul and key bases. With the heavy losses at the Battle of Midway, the Japanese commit submarines to attack the long American logistic lines across the Pacific, with shorter range submarines kept in reserve to support operations. The four old battleships Ise, Hyuga, Fuso, and Yamashiro are kept as a fleet in being at several important islands such as Rabul, and are converted into floating fortresses, forcing the Americans to have to destroy these heavily armored units before attempting an invasion of these islands. Realizing their codes have been broken by the American deception at Midway, the Japanese change their codes, although keeping their old ones for deception operations. Despite priority given to escort ships, to rebuild the lost carrier forces, the Japanese decide to convert the Shinano and Ibuki into aircraft carriers, along with speeding up the construction of the Taiho. To not lower pilot quality and train enough pilots to man these new carriers, they adopt a more efficient pilot training program based on the American system. To defend better against American aircraft and submarine attacks on important supply ships and troop transports, they also adopt the convoy system, allowing more ships to be defended by less escorts than sailing separately, along with committing all four Kongo class battleships for particularly large and important convoys. With peace achieved with Britain, including Australia and New Zealand, the Japanese can transfer forces from New Guinea to other Pacific islands. Realizing an opportunity to lure the Americans into a successful battle while evacuating from New Guinea, the Japanese use their old codes saying that two fleet carriers and one light carrier will be covering the evacuation from New Guinea. What was transmitted in the new codes, however, was that the carrier forces were a decoy, which would allow the Japanese battleships Yamato, Nagato, Mutsu, and Musashi to destroy the American carriers, making up for the loss at Midway. The pilots in this battle are also tasked with learning American formations and tactics, reporting them back to the carriers. This would allow the Japanese to devise counterstrategies against the Americans. The Americans, meanwhile, hope to destroy the remainder of the Japanese carrier force, knowing that the new Essex class carriers are only months away.

Chapter 4: Technology and Zombies

After digging in on the Don and Volga rivers, the Axis await the massive Soviet counteroffensive, aimed at cutting off the Sixth Army on the Volga. The main brunt of the assault will fall on the weaker Romanian and Hungarian armies, with lower morale and weaker equipment than their German counterparts. The offensive initially opens to great success, smashing the Second Hungarian Army along the Don and the Fourth Romanian Army in the Caucasus, while diversion attacks are launched against the German First Panzer and Seventeenth Armies in the Caucasus, and the German Second and Fourth Panzer Armies on the Don. Attacks aimed at pinning down the German Sixth Army on the Volga are also launched. Despite a breakthrough achieved and the Second Hungarian and Fourth Romanian Armies fleeing, German divisions transferred from Army Group Center, the transfer of one corps from the Italian Eighth Army, Axis air superiority, and zombie and anti-Soviet resistance groups behind the front line halt the Soviet pincers past Elista in the south and Kotelnikov in the north. However, towards the end of the campaign, the Soviet Z-4 explosive turns the tide in the war against the zombies, freeing up enormous amounts of men to increase pressure against the German Fourth Panzer and Second Armies, and with the threat of zombies in the rear greatly subsided, the Soviets break through despite being unable to capture Voronezh, forcing the remnants of the Second Hungarian and Fourth Romanian Armies to stabilize the front, which the Soviets exploited by connecting the two pincers against the Third Romanian Army, completely destroying it, cutting off the German Sixth Army on the Volga. Meanwhile, as Rommel gave up the last parts of western Libya, Army Group Africa launched a massive attack against inexperienced American forces, and well supplied without Malta's interdiction, were able to advance to Algiers. Around the same time, the first German zombie mind control rays arrived in Tunisia, allowing Rommel to redirect the vast amounts of zombies created in his victory in Algeria to stabilize the front in Tunisia, allowing him to move regular forces against the British on the Mareth Line. After the end of the Soviet counteroffensive, the newly created Army Group Don, consisting of the remaining Romanian and Hungarian forces, seven divisions of the Italian Eighth Army, and spearheaded by the German Fourth Panzer Army, launched an offensive to relieve the encircled German Sixth Army. The offensive met strong Soviet resistance but was eventually able to break through to the Volga, allowing the Fourth Panzer Army to expand the corridor southwards and join the First Panzer Army's renewed offensive south to recapture Gronzy and break into Baku once and for all. As construction on the aircraft carriers Graf Zepplin and the Weser continued, a change in German naval codes forced the Allies to divert essential resources from the Pacific to the Atlantic to combat the German U-boats. The Gneisnau's planned repair and upgrading continued, becoming a major threat to the vital Artic Convoys. Around the same time the German First Panzer Army recaptured Gronzy, the first German zombie mind control rays on the Eastern Front were used with devastating effect against the Soviet armies on the Don, and with the high casualties the Soviets took feeding the zombie numbers, the zombies were able to push the Soviet past the Don back to Germany's former positions. Meanwhile, the German Second Army and part of the German Sixth Army, supported by Romanian, Italian, and Hungarian troops, started expanding the corridor established to the Volga northwards, pushing the Soviets to the Don as well. However, increasing Soviet resistance in the Fourth Panzer Army's drive to Baku and logistics problems for the Axis allowed the Soviets to launch their first successful summer offensive, halting the Axis advance to Baku cold and protecting Baku from falling into German hands. Realizing the inability to capture the oil fields, Hitler orders every available German aircraft to bomb Baku as much as possible, to deny the oil fields to the Soviets. However, strong Soviet resistance prevent the near destruction of the oil facilities, despite significant damage, which would cut Soviet oil production, in conjunction with the fall of Maykop and Gronzy, by 30%. The large civilian casualties in the Siege of Leningrad provide the best place to station new zombie mind control rays, crushing the Soviet defense as street after street are fought over, each zombie taking one person with them, therefore providing an endless supply of manpower. By the end of the summer of 1943, Leningrad had been captured, freeing up enormous amounts of German troops for the deadliest Soviet offensive yet. However, with strong reinforcements from the Far East, the British were able to drive the Axis past the Mareth Line, only halting after Tunis had been captured. With the Americans recapturing the rest of Algeria and beginning to push along the coast of Tunisia, realizing that the situation is untenable, Rommel withdraws from southern Tunisia and launches a counterattack against the Americans to pin down their forces. The main assault is launched against the British to reach Tunis. This would buy enough time for large amounts of his forces to be evacuated by air and sea, just as the Americans, who have recovered from their defeat in Algeria, break through around the same time as the first Z.I.B.R.A suits and chainsaw tanks are produced.

Chapter 5: Death to The Zombies!

The Soviet 1943 winter offensive was aimed at driving through the sector of the Don held by zombies, therefore cutting off large amounts of forces in the eastern sector of the Don and the Volga, as well as recapturing Smolensk, therefore denying the Axis the most direct route to Moscow. After the success of these two offensives, to secure more oil supplies after the massed Axis bombing attacks on Baku, a drive to recapture Gronzy, Maykop, and Rostov would commence. With Z-4 explosives mass produced, the Soviets punched through the zombies, and despite anti-Soviet resistance in the rear as well as large amounts of zombies created due to losses, the Soviets punched through the front line, forcing the Axis to move the German Second Army as well as divisions transferred from Army Group North's Leningrad sector and the Army Group Center to hold the line. Despite the halting of the Soviet advance, the assault was quickly moved eastwards, rapidly destroying all Hungarian and Romanian forces, and decimating most of the Italian Eighth Army, leaving only the Alpini troops fighting in the Caucasus mountains left on the Eastern Front. The transfer of enormous amounts of zombies from the western sector of the Don and the large amounts of zombies created after the decimating of Italian, Romanian, and Hungarian armies, however, was able to cover the evacuation of the German Sixth Army from the Volga before the zombies were destroyed. Meanwhile, the Soviets were able to capture Smolensk, and despite supply problems due to the loss of large amounts of Soviet oil and the interdiction of supplies along the Volga, the Soviets pushed back the German Fourth Panzer and First Panzer Armies, recapturing Gronzy, but the arrival of the German Sixth Army enabled Germany to slow down the Soviet attacks against Maykop and eventually stopped them due to large amounts of zombie activity against the Soviet forces attacking directly on the other side of the frontline. Towards the end of the campaign in 1944, the Allies launched the invasion of Sardinia and Corsica, rapidly destroying the small Axis forces stationed there, and by the time the Allies landed in Anzio, the Soviets simultaneously destroyed the German Seventeenth Army, except for the Italian Alpini, which, despite several years of hard fighting and heavy casualties, had one division's worth of men able to escape. By the end of the winter of 1943-1944, the depleted Fourth Panzer and First Panzer Armies, realizing that their current positions are untenable, are transferred to hold the line left by the German Second Army's transfer to Italy, leaving the German Sixth Army with a long salient ending at Maykop. The remnants of the Italian Alpini forces are also recalled to Italy for the final defense of the homeland. Despite these odds, Mussolini continues to control Italy as the Allies fight north to Rome. With their forces decimated, the Axis are no longer to launch a large-scale offensive on the Eastern Front, instead digging in to defend against the massive Soviet summer offensive against Ukraine, Belarus, and Leningrad, as most damage in Baku has been repaired.

Chapter 6: Zombie Hopping

Off New Guinea, American carrier aircraft spot several Japanese transports, escorting destroyers, and cruisers, as well as the carriers intelligence told them about. Soon, the carriers Enterprise, Saratoga, Hornet, and Wasp launch their carrier aircraft, while the Ryujo, Shokaku and Zuikaku launch their carrier aircraft around the same time, supported by land-based aircraft from New Guinea, in a head on engagement. Outnumbered, the Ryujo is sunk, while the Shokaku takes heavy damage, with the Zuikaku taking many hits and Japanese aircraft concentrate on the Hornet, avenging the Doolittle Raid. However, as this air battle is taking place, the battleships Yamato, Musashi, Nagato, and Mutsu, supported by several cruisers and destroyers, are able to approach the American carriers unknown to almost point-blank range. After the battleships align to shoot all main guns at once, a massive salvo, aimed at the Enterprise and Saratoga, cripple both ships, just as the Wasp is torpedoed by supporting submarines.

This diverts large amounts of American aircraft to attack the two battleships, allowing Japanese aircraft and submarines to deal the fatal blows on the Enterprise, while the Yamato, Nagato, the Mustu, and the Musashi finish off the Saratoga, and despite American efforts, is sunk. As the battleships maneuver to attack the Hornet, suddenly, the Shokaku explodes by American aircraft. In fierce revenge for the loss of one of Japan's most modern carriers, the Saratoga is quickly sunk, with Japanese cruisers and destroyers using their long lance torpedoes to devastate the American escorts. As the Wasp tries to limp back to base to tell the tale of this cunning deception, it is hit by several attacks of the Yamato and the Musashi, along with torpedoes from submarines. Realizing the situation is hopeless, the ship is scuttled. The defeat at Midway is avenged, and America's entire carrier force sunk, but at a heavy cost. Of the three great carrier battles fought, five Japanese fleet carriers and two light carriers are lost for six American fleet carriers. Japanese aircraft and pilots have taken a heavy blow as well, with the few survivors reporting the aerial tactics of the Americans. With the Zuikaku under repairs, as the veterans rest and train new pilots, other Japanese officers devise tactics to counter the Americans. With the forces stationed in New Guinea transferred to the Marshall and Gilbert islands, the Japanese Army, with new confidence after the end of the draining Burma campaign and the successful evacuation of New Guinea, launches Operation Ichi-Go, connecting the areas captured in Southeast Asia to the Japanese forces in China, allowing for resources to flow more easily to the home islands. Despite the loss of their carrier forces and the loss of supplies via the Japanese submarine campaign, the Americans advance and land in the Marshalls and Giberts and despite heavy casualties, push through. By the end of 1943, the Allies have captured the Marshalls, the Gilberts, the Aleutians, Ulithi Atoll in the Caroline Islands, as well as the Solomons. At the start of 1944, the Allies launch a massive attack against Rabul, aimed at drawing the IJN into a decisive battle and neutralize the important base of Rabul. Meanwhile, over the course of the rest of

1942 and 1943, the IJN rebuilt their carrier forces, amassing a large force of five fleet carriers and four light carriers. This was opposed however, by seven light carriers and five fleet carriers of the US navy. To balance against American forces, however, the Japanese move large amounts of land-based aircraft, along with their entire battleship force, to Rabul, finding out American intentions after large amounts of ships were spotted preparing for the invasion. The Japanese, who have been using their old codes throughout 1943, decide to use their old codes to deceive the US navy and defeat them piecemeal. Despite being a bit skeptical of the report that all of Japan's battleships, 12 in total, are moving in directions very far from each other to intercept the invasion, carrier aircraft discover the truth. Hoping to demonstrate to the admirals he had been fighting with for years over the use of carriers instead of battleships, the commander of the Fast Carrier Task Force, Marc A. Mitscher, orders his aircraft to launch a massive attack against the slow-moving Japanese battleships. Due to the distance between both battleship forces, two task groups consisting of two fleet carriers and two light carriers, move in separate directions, launching their vast swarms of aircraft against the two battleship forces. Each one consists of two Kongo class battleships, one Fuso class, one Ise class, one Nagato class, and one Yamato class battleship. Within an hour, the lightly armored Kongo class battleships sink, while the obsolete Fuso and Ise class battleships take large amounts of damage. At this point, in the attack against the battleships west of the American invading force, American aircraft suddenly spot many Japanese aircraft moving against the American carriers. With the focus of the carriers now on the Japanese carriers, the Ryuho and Zuiho is sunk, and the Chitose and Chiyoda are heavily crippled, but overwhelmed, all-American carriers are sunk. In the air battle, American pilots are shocked to see Japanese pilots using their tactics against them, leading to the destruction of many American aircraft. Realizing that the Japanese carriers are going to move out against the American carriers that are attacking the eastern Japanese battleship force, a third task force, consisting of one fleet carrier and three light carriers, is moved eastward to support that assault. By the time the Japanese carriers arrive, the Musashi is in flames, with the Mutsu slowly listing and all other ships sunk. Realizing that they are outnumbered, the Japanese launch all land-based aircraft on Rabul and move all submarines to sink the American carriers. In the ensuring air battle, one fleet carrier and three light carriers are sunk, two light carriers and one fleet carrier are crippled, and one fleet carrier is moderately damaged on the American side, with the Hiyo, Junyo, and Zuikaku heavily crippled, the Shinano, Mushashi, and Mutsu sunk, and the Taiho taking moderate damage. The carefully maneuvered Japanese submarines, however, suddenly launch all their torpedoes, salvo after salvo, sinking two American light carriers and one fleet carrier. As the crippled Essex limps back to the invasion fleet, the damaged Yamato, who continued moving towards the invasion fleet, successfully places, at very long range, a fatal hit, causing the last American carrier in the Pacific to explode. Angered at the loss of all their carriers, and sighting the

Yamato, the battleships Iowa and the New Jersey chase the Yamato. With superior speed, the two battleships easily catch up with the Yamato, destroying it, withering under the powerful fire of both the Iowa and the New Jersey, but damaging both. Despite a strong bombardment and complete Allied air superiority due to the Japanese withdrawal of all land-based aircraft and non-combat personnel such as engineers from Rabul, the cunning and new Japanese tactic of keeping large amounts of zombies in reserve as the regular soldiers destroyed the American chainsaw tanks, and once all regular soldiers are dead, the zombies, kept in reserve inside underground tunnels, pounce on the Americans, causing heavy casualties on the US troops.

Chapter 7: Zombie Breakthrough

In early 1943, Hitler, realizing that the Axis would need all strength possible to combat the growing Soviet strength on the Eastern Front, orders the construction of the Panther-Wotan line along the Dnieper, stretching north across the entire Eastern front, and even to the entrance to the Crimea from Ukraine. More importantly, Hitler declares total war, moving all workers into the war industry, aimed at producing as much equipment as possible. However, as the Anglo-American bombing intensified, large amounts of zombies were created, who couldn't be moved due to bombing of the zombie mind control way towers. However, anticipating a need for such units, German scientists also began developing a special underground version of the zombie mind control rays, simultaneously with the tower version, which is first used to move the large amounts of zombies created in the Anglo-American bombing campaign to Italy. In the spring of 1944, the German Sixth Army was involved in several vicious defensive battles against the Soviets over Maykop, ending in the near destruction of the army as it withdrew from the salient and dissolved units sent to rebuild other armies. Meanwhile, the battered German Fourth Panzer Army is dissolved, with the units being sent to rebuild, along with reinforcements arriving, to rebuild the First, Second, and Third Panzer Armies back to full strength. These three Panzer armies are withdrawn from the large German southern salient to the Dnieper, leaving infantry divisions to take over the defense of the area. In the central sector of the front, the Russian Liberation Army grew over the past year to the size of an Army Group, allowing all of Army Group Center to transfer southwards. Since this was an uneventful area of the Eastern Front, the Russian Liberation Army established many anti Soviet contacts behind the Soviet front line. As expected, the Soviet summer offensive fell against Leningrad and the southern sector, rapidly liberating Leningrad and shattering the Axis forces, pushing them past the Donets River. However, catching the Soviet forces overextended, just as they crossed the entrance to the Crimea, the three Panzer armies caught the Soviets by surprise, pushing all the way back to the Donets River. Despite this loss, the Soviets were able to push hard against the Panzer armies, ending in a pocket engulfing all of them, leaving the southern sector of the Eastern Front undefended and the Soviets reaching the Dnieper and clearing out the Crimea. While these battles were happening, after having their suspicions confirmed that the main brunt of the Soviet offensive would be aimed at Ukraine, the Russian Liberation Army, equipped with the large amounts of equipment built by Germany after the launch of the total war campaign, launched a massive offensive against Moscow, and with large amounts of Red Army defections and help by anti-Soviet resistance groups, capture Smolensk quickly, pushing hard against Moscow. Despite long and extended flanks, the Russian Liberation Army brush aside any Soviet resistance put up, arriving at the gates of Moscow as the Soviets transfer as many men as possible from the Far East. Before the offensive could continue, however, a massive attack launched on the flanks by the Soviets, using forces transferred from the northern and southern sectors, was launched, and despite defections by the Red Army troops, the Russian Liberation Army is forced to redirect reserves to defend the flanks, just as anti-Soviet partisan groups in Moscow are able to sabotage Stalin's train out of Moscow, assassinating him and most of the government leadership. The resulting disarray of Red Army allows the Russian Liberation Army to capture Moscow after a bitter street fight, even with large amounts of zombies crawling at the rear. A military dominated government under Zhukov rises to power but is unpopular as mass civil unrest in the wake of Stalin's death and the Russian Liberation Army's hopeful message threaten to depose the Soviet government once and for all. To rebuild public morale and assure the public of the strength of the Soviet Union, even after Moscow's fall, a massive assault is launched on the Dnieper, but is beaten off after enormous casualties on both sides by the newly raised First, Second, and Third Hungarian Armies, the Fourth Romanian Army, and supported by the newly formed

German Fifth Panzer Army. The fortifications along the Dnieper proved decisive, but a bigger impact was the large amounts of zombies created after the past offensives of the year, forcing the Soviets, even with Z-4 explosives, to dedicate large amounts of units to wipe them out. Both sides are far too exhausted for further offensive operations, as the Russian Liberation Army consolidates their new gains, using new underground zombie mind control rays to spread havoc deep into Soviet land, and logistics and supply lines are secured.

Chapter 8: The Zombie's European War

While events unfolded on the Eastern Front, the Western Allies launched enormous offensives against Axis forces in France and Italy, landing in France and sweeping aside the meager resistance, liberating all of France, Belgium, Luxembourg, and The Netherlands by the end of the year, while the vast amounts of zombies created in the rear are easily destroyed by hunter groups equipped with chainsaw tanks and Z.I.B.R.A suits. In Italy, the Allies launch a simultaneous offensive, pushing north, capturing all of Italy, only stopping at Yugoslavia. As the winter of 1944 sets in, the Russian Liberation Army launches a massive assault pushing against the new Soviet capital, Kuibyshev. However, as the Russian Liberation Army advanced, the Red Army, having destroyed all zombies behind the frontline allowing for reinforcement of the attacking forces, launched a winter assault against the Dnieper, which succeeded, even with German zombie mind control rays using large amounts of zombies as a reserve, as all regular German reinforcements are rushed to the Western Front. With the Red Army having destroyed the Fourth Romanian and Third Hungarian Armies, easily chasing the battered First and Second Hungarian Armies encircling and destroying them, leaving the understrength German Fifth Panzer Army to withdraw into Romania, leaving the Soviets to liberate all of Ukraine. However, with the Russian Liberation Army's advance stopped by Soviet forces pulled from the northern sector of the front, an offensive launched in the early months of 1945 at the northern and southern parts of the Eastern Front by the Russian Liberation Army succeeded in pushing the Soviets out of Ukraine and, in conjunction with Finnish forces, recapturing Leningrad. With the threat on the Eastern Front now safe, the German Fifth Panzer Army is dissolved, with the units sent to the newly reactivated First, Second, and Third Panzer Armies on the Western Front. By the beginning of 1945, a meeting by Hitler and the leadership of the Russian Liberation Army agree that the Russian Liberation Army should solely hold the line on the Eastern

Front while Germany focuses on fighting the Western Allies to a standstill. Towards the end of the winter campaign, the Soviets, with enormous amounts of Far Eastern units transferred, launches a counterattack, pushing the Russian Liberation Army back to their starting positions. By the start of spring 1945, the Russian Liberation Army digs in, rebuilding the southern part of the Panther-Wotan line, and using large amounts of zombies in reserve to help cover retreats when necessary. A massive problem to the Soviet Union's preparations for their 1945 summer offensive, and a serious worry, was when the Japanese, viewing the large amounts of troop movements from the Far East, inform the Soviets that their non-aggression pact would not be renewed. Zombie attacks also cause some disruptions to preparations but are overall not decisive. However, in the spring of 1945, zombies created from the bombing of Baku, the battles on the southern sector of the Eastern Front, and the Russian Liberation Army's drive on Kuibyshev invade Turkey. Overwhelmed by sheer numbers, and lacking anti-zombie equipment, Turkey becomes a largely controlled zombie area. In 1945, the Western Allies launch powerful assaults on the Siegfried Line and the hurriedly built Alpine Line in Austria, dissolving into steady attritional fighting, although a lunge towards Turkey through liberating Albania and Greece is successful. The invasion of zombie-controlled Turkey, however, took until the end of the year for a decisive victory by American chainsaw tanks and British Z.I.B.R.A suit equipped assault teams, but even then, large amounts of clean-up operations are required. By the summer of 1945, the Soviets launch an enormous attack, easily punching through the Russian Liberation Army lines, although the use of covering forces in the form of zombies allow the Russian Liberation Army to fall back to the Panther-Wotan Line. However, the Soviets also punched through that by the end of the year, reaching the Soviet Union's 1940 borders, driving the Finnish troops back to their 1940 borders, except for Romania. Despite most of the Russian Liberation Army annihilated, the incoming zombie storm, heavy casualties taken in the drive to the 1940 borders over the summer, continuing into winter, a Japanese invasion of the Soviet Union and anti-Soviet groups launching a coordinated uprising, all reduced Soviet manpower levels massively. This led to Zhukov decided to sign a peace treaty with the Axis in early 1946, with the terms being that the Germans will take control of Ukraine, eastern Poland, all three of the Baltic States, Belarus, and that German companies will be available to access Soviet oil fields in Baku, Gronzy, and Maykop.

Chapter 9: Zombie Power

As promised, Belarus, the Baltic States, and Ukraine are converted into individual self-governing regions, although they are supported and have strong relations with Germany. Finland also receives all the land lost in the Winter War. Instead of attacking the oilfields as some Allied planners suggested in 1944, enormous amounts of resources were used against Germany's ball bearings industry, causing enormous amounts of damage. The offensive produced minimal results, however, as the Germans built up large reserves of ball bearings before the campaign from surplus production and imported large amounts of ball bearings from Sweden and Switzerland. With Germany and Romania's oil industries running at full capacity, the Luftwaffe, was able to use their new ME 262 jet fighters to their full capacity, shooting down large numbers of Allied aircraft, although sheer Allied numbers allowed for continued bombing of the ball bearings industry. In preparation as fallback positions, as the fighting around the Siegfried Line raged,

Germany produced an additional defensive line along the Rhine, with priority being given to the sector facing France, as the Siegfried Line in this area was being the most strained than in sectors more in the northern part of the line facing Belgium, Luxembourg, and the Netherlands. Throughout 1945, Germany continued to rebuild their Panzer forces in reserve, eventually being able to reactivate the Fourth Panzer Army. This industrial production of tanks was aided by the complete diversion of resources from submarine warfare at the end of 1943, by which point, despite the Germans changing their codes, the Allies were able to win the Battle Of The Atlantic by sheer numbers. The Siegfried Line facing France was broken near the beginning of winter, although the northern sector withstood heavy British attacks. Despite the Rhine Line still requiring a few more months to complete, the German Army was forced to fall back to the line, which the Allies couldn't break through due to diversion of resources for an offensive against the Alps Line, as attacks largely petered out over the summer due to a diversion of resources to invade Bulgaria, which proved tougher than expected, as five Bulgarian armies, fierce and ready to defend their homeland, slowed the Allied advance that began in the summer, finally being finished off in the winter. As resources were moved to assault the Alps Line one final time before the winter made operations impossible, a weak offensive against Romania was stopped by the Romanian First Army. Despite almost breaking, the Alps Line held on, preventing the Allies from reaching important industrial targets in southern Germany and outflanking the German defenses on the Rhine Line. Meanwhile, at sea in 1945, Germany, realizing that a decisive naval battle to restore morale for the Axis and drop morale for the Allies, orders all remaining heavy surface units, four heavy cruisers, three battleships, two fleet carriers, four light carriers, and almost all the Kriegsmarine's remaining destroyers, are to sortie to destroy British ships blockading the Norwegian coast aimed at drawing out and destroying all remaining German surface units. The British forces the Germans met consisted of the battleship Vanguard, whose construction was accelerated as much as possible, coming at the expense of bombing programs, four aircraft carriers, twelve heavy cruisers, and four battleships, as many destroyers as the Germans brought, and two American battleships. As the Germans were able to keep this mobilization of naval units very secretive despite the amounts of ships involved, in a surprise attack by the aircraft carriers that caught all four carriers in between rotations of combat air patrol, despite intense anti-aircraft fire resulting in the destruction of nearly all German aircraft, the massive explosions of the aircraft carriers with many aircraft and stocks of fuel cause four British aircraft carriers, two heavy cruisers, and one American battleship to be sunk, two British heavy cruisers, and one American battleship crippled forcing them to turn back to port, and two British battleships are damaged. As the German surface fleet neared the British fleets, a reconnaissance aircraft spotted four German light aircraft carriers. Hoping to get revenge on the German carriers, the two damaged British battleships move towards the carriers to attack. As the German surface fleet approaches the rest of British fleet, all ships, who have numerical equality, attack each other in several nearly equal battles. All British destroyers attack an equal number of German destroyers in many one-to-one skirmishes, the Tirpitz taking on the Vanguard, the Gneisenau taking on the King George V, the Scharnhorst being swarmed by three heavy cruisers, and all four German heavy cruisers engaging in battles with equal amounts of Allied heavy cruisers. After a very tough battle, the Tirpitz finally destroys the Vanguard, although the Tirpitz itself is crippled. Despite incredible British resistance, the Gneisenau sinks the King George V, but is also nearly sunk. While the Scharnhorst sinks two heavy cruisers, the final one gains a decisive torpedo blow on the Scharnhorst but is able to damage the cruiser enough to be sunk by the German ships Deutschland and Admiral Scheer, who have narrowly beaten their own cruisers, without much damage. As the two British battleships approach the four German light carriers, it is discovered they are a decoy, without any aircraft, as all remaining naval aircraft are based on the Graf Zeppelin. After the easy destruction of these ships, the last victory of the Luftwaffe cripple both British battleships, with a newly borrowed tactic from the Japanese of crashing into ships if the aircraft is damaged beyond repair, a tactic that gives devastating results due to the high accuracy of these attacks. In the last use of the German aircraft carriers, naval aircraft, using the same tactic that the land-based Luftwaffe used earlier against the two British battleships, sinking them. While this duel in the north took place, Admiral Hipper and the Prinz Eugen were able to prevail against the British heavy cruisers attacking them, although in the end, all German heavy cruisers are damaged, with the Admiral Hipper and the Prinz Eugen being more damaged than the other two. The British and German destroyer battles, with numbers being exactly equal, depended mostly on luck, with both sides winning half of the battles each, although all surviving ships are crippled. As the German ships move back to base, a massive Allied air attack sinks the fleet carriers I and Graf Zeppelin, brushing aside any air cover, destroying the remainder of

Germany's carrier force, destroying all German light cruisers anchored in port, exploding them all, all four German heavy cruisers, the Gneisenau, and all remaining destroyers. The crippled Tirpitz, however, is untouched, sails back to the German naval base of Kiel.

Chapter 10: Land of the Zombies

With the Russian Liberation Army almost annihilated, all remaining equipment, largely German made, but also consisting of many captured pieces of Soviet equipment, are turned over to Germany, helping rebuild the reactivated Fourth Panzer Army to full strength. While Germans man most pieces of equipment, anti-capitalist volunteers man some of them. These volunteers are concentrated in one volunteer infantry division. They are rushed to the frontline on the Rhine Line, which is not bombed to support the evidently failing ball bearings campaign despite American army appeals. The division was able to halt an Allied breakthrough on the line, around the same time the Allies launched their final assault on the Alps Line. Despite losing large amounts of men which led to the division converting to a regiment and attached to a regular German infantry division, the division was able to delay the Allied advance long enough for German reinforcements to arrive, preventing a crisis. The Allied assault on the Alps Line, despite impressive numbers and coming very close to victory, failed, and just as attack ended, the British were able to finally breakthrough the German Siegfried Line facing Luxembourg. However, the sector facing Belgium and the Netherlands is unbroken. Realizing the manpower shortage facing Germany, Hitler, hoping to launch one final offensive to compel the Allies to negotiate a peace treaty, creates a plan for an offensive in Belgium, spearheaded by the First, Second, and Third Panzer Armies, supported by the newly reactivated Sixth Army, and the First, Fifthteenth, and Seventh Armies. A secondary offensive, spearheaded by the Fourth Panzer Army and supported by the newly reactivated Second Army, previously destroyed in Italy, will also be launched. As the winter of 1945 drew closer, the Allies invaded Hungary, which, after losing all armies in the battles on the Eastern Front, quickly collapses, followed by Slovakia. With their southeastern flank exposed, German forces defending on the Alpine Line are redirected, but an Allied exploitation of this diversion is slow, as the cold of the Alps in the winter sets in. As the Yugoslavian government in exile tries to reinstate order in Yugoslavia, a massive uprising by the Communist partisans erupts into full scale war, forcing the Allies to divert large amounts of resources fighting on the Siegfried Line, particularly in the Ardennes sector, to support the anticommunist Yugoslavian government. Despite Allied success, the fast partisans, supported by most of the population, escaped being destroyed, and an agreement in early 1946 was achieved where the political issue will be ignored until the defeat of the Axis, with the communists providing the First, Second, and Third Yugoslavian Armies. To conserve as much manpower and heavy equipment for the final offensive, the cunning use of zombie mind control rays allowed German troops to defend the Siegfried, Rhine, and Alps Lines to keep fighting even when killed, allowing Germany to have twice the number of troops than deployed. The Germans noticed the siphoning of forces to Yugoslavia, and as the winter is forecasted to be particularly long this year, which would prevent the Allies from achieving air superiority. The First and Second Panzer Armies will launch a pincer movement through the lightly defended Ardennes towards Antwerp, cutting off British forces in the Netherlands fighting along the Siegfried Line which would be destroyed by forces on the Siegfried Line and the First and Seventh Armies, and encircling troops southeast of Antwerp, which will be destroyed by the Sixth Army. The Third Panzer Army, meanwhile, will launch an offensive, driving towards Brussels and tying down Allied reserves. The Fifthteenth and Sixth Armies will be used to safeguard the western flank, while the First and Seventh Armies will cover the eastern flanks before being released to wipe out the British forces in the Netherlands. A secondary offensive, spearheaded by the Fourth Panzer Army, with support by the newly reactivated Second Army, will also be launched around the same time, cutting off and encircling the American forces attacking the Rhine Line, trapping them between the formidable German defenses of the Rhine Line and the Fourth Panzer and Second Armies. They would be manning a hurriedly rebuilt Siegfried

Line, using guns, metal, and other things from the battleship Tripitz, which, after being determined that the cost of repairing it would outweigh the benefits, is scrapped, and the Kriegsmarine, lacking few ships, is disbanded, with most personnel being transferred to the army, retrained and used as infantry to bolster Germany's dwindling manpower reserves. All remaining German ships, including a few submarines and coastal defense vessels, such as E-boats, are reassigned to be under the direct command of armed forces. The offensive, supplied with enough fuel to drive most of the way towards the objectives of Antwerp and Brussels, catches the Allied forces by surprise, moving rapidly enough to capture enough fuel to reach Antwerp, and allowing the First Panzer Army to dispatch a corps to encircle and destroy the American defenders in Bastogne, which, despite fierce defense, is destroyed. The advance moved on schedule, although the dispatching of the First Panzer Army's corps slowed the advance in the east a little, but the Second Panzer Army's success allowed it to destroy vast amounts of Allied units in the drive towards Antwerp, even as the Allies regrouped and put up increasing resistance. Near the outskirts of Antwerp, however, the Second Panzer Army got bogged down, with the First Panzer Army reaching the same positions a few days later and being stopped. In the attack to Brussels, the Third Panzer Army, after initial gains, transferred to join the Second Panzer Army in a final attack against Antwerp after moving halfway to Brussels. The Allies, as expected, devoted more resources blunting the Third Panzer Army's advance, but by the time reinforcements arrived, the Third Panzer Army had already transferred, and they were moved south to help cut off and destroy the Fourth Panzer Army, which was able to reach most of the way to the Swiss border, with no sign of stopping. With the bulk of the Third Panzer Army behind it, and the winter weather lasting longer than expected, a final breakthrough against Antwerp succeeded, and by the start of 1946, after a long and grueling street battle, Antwerp fell with enormous amounts of supplies captured, with the First Panzer Army reaching the area the same day. Large amounts of American troops, without supply, were cut off, as were British troops in the Netherlands. As planned, the Sixth Army moved in to destroy the Allied armies in the pocket, while the Seventh and First Armies, supported by the First Panzer Army, in conjunction with forces on the Siegfried Line, invaded the Netherlands. With the Sixth Army making slower progress than expected, and signs of the weather clearing soon, the Second Panzer Army is moved southwards to support the offensive, while the Third Panzer Army is moved to defend the northern western part of the bulge. In the south, the Fourth Panzer Army succeeded in reaching the Swiss border, but American reinforcements were able to open a narrow corridor to the encirclement, as most American reinforcements were again diverted northwards, losing critical time, to open a corridor to trapped British forces in the Netherlands. Throughout most of the winter, the Luftwaffe conserved as many resources as possible, and while this had a negative impact on industry, by the time the skies cleared in the first months of 1946, the Luftwaffe launched their final operation, gaining temporary and local air superiority over the Fourth Panzer and Second Armies, allowing them to close the corridor and link up with forces that attacked from the Rhine Line in the final days of 1945. With a less pressing need for aircraft in the northern sector, air parity was achieved over the Netherlands and the pocket in eastern Belgium, allowing for the destruction of both forces. With the British forces rapidly eroding in northwestern Netherlands, a massive Allied counteroffensive, supported by large amounts of aircraft that defeated the Luftwaffe in the air, pushed back against the Third Panzer and Fifteenth Armies, but the transfer of the First Panzer Army and the Sixth Army prevented a collapse, although the German forces were depleted enough that the Sixth Army was once again dissolved to support the precarious Fifteenth Army. By the time Allied forces reconquered all of Belgium, including Antwerp, and destroyed the Third and First Panzer Armies, all British forces in the Netherlands and American forces in the encirclement near the Rhine and Siegfried Lines were destroyed, and the Luftwaffe was almost destroyed by the attrition that the campaign entailed. In a surprise move, Allied forces land in Norway, and despite fierce German defenses, the Allies break through, causing Finland to sue for peace. With Allied forces punching through the Siegfried Line, the Netherlands, and a full advance through the Alps Line and Poland in the summer of 1946, the Allies finally accept German peace offers, as Poland, Denmark and Czechoslovakia are liberated, Romania conquered, and the Rhine Line broken in the beginning of winter of 1946. Despite a massive German defeat, the final German offensive was successful, as it caused havoc for the Allies and made Allied planners realize that any invasion of Germany would be at an enormous cost in blood. The peace treaty is less harsh than the Treaty of Versailles and details that Germany will give up all foreign conquered territories, including Austria and Sudetenland, but will claim back the Polish Corridor, although Poland will claim Konigsberg and the surrounding area, allowing for Poland to continue to have a coast without interrupting a German land link to East Prussia. Alsace-Lorraine and all other territories lost in World War 1 will stay lost, and the Saar territory will be given back to Germany. The Nazi regime, however, is allowed to survive. No economic reparations are required, and the required reparations after World War 1 of the A and B bonds are cut in half, with the C bonds not required at all, to help Germany focus on debt from both world wars and before them. With the war in Europe over, and bitter at the Soviet Union's peace treaty with Germany, the Western Allies back the Yugoslavian government in exile against the Yugoslavian communists, leading to a prolonged campaign lasting until 1950, when the last holdout was captured, and Tito accidentally killed.

Chapter 11: Battleships, Cruisers, And Zombies

After the victory at Rabul, the Allies, hoping to prevent a Japanese counterattack, invade the rest of New Britain and begin preparations of the invasion of the Marianas. The New Britain campaign causes heavy casualties, and the same tactic used at Rabul is also used on the Marianas, where the Japanese move all available forces to the three islands of Tinian, Saipan, and Guam, which happen to be the islands the Americans are assaulting, causing heavy casualties. Due to the IJN still recovering from the losses inflicted off Rabul, the landings were unopposed by the navy, as were the landings at Iwo Jima and Rota Island. Despite this, the army was able to inflict high casualties on the Americans, and the bombing of Japan accelerated, causing problems to Japanese war production. Realizing that Truk was untenable, the Japanese evacuated all aircraft, naval ships, and army units from the island, redeploying them to heavily reinforce the defenses on Okinawa. With almost no units left on Truk, the bombing of the island by American aircraft caused little damage. As the winter of 1944 approached, the Allies had enough forces to launch one more campaign before the end of the year. Okinawa was chosen, but as the Japanese were able to construct very well dug in defenses, reinforced by enormous amounts of forces from garrisons of Truk and Southeast Asia, as well as newly raised forces from the home islands, the Allies took large amounts of casualties, with the battle lasting well into 1945, as zombies attacked the American rear, and large amounts of zombies created from the bombing campaign of the home islands, released towards the end of the battle, delayed the end of the campaign until summer 1945. Meanwhile, as the dawn of 1945 emerged, an argument over whether Formosa or the Philippines should be invaded started throughout the Allied high command, as both sectors are crucial to intercepting and destroying Japanese supply ships more effectively, as despite increasing American submarine success, more than half of Japanese convoys were able to arrive at the home islands. Knowing that support for the Pacific

War is lowering after the heavy casualties incurred at Okinawa and Rabul in particular, and the commitment of forces to Okinawa, meant that resources were insufficient for invasions both areas. While the debate continued, following the naval battle off Rabul, the Japanese dedicated as many resources as possible to building three Unryu class fleet carriers as well as training the pilots as efficiently and as well as possible for the carriers. The heavily damaged Ise and Fuso are scrapped to support this program, leaving the Nagato as the only battleship of the IJN, and resources from escort production are diverted to the construction of the carriers. As Soviet resources are siphoned off westward, including the First and Second Red Banner Armies, the Japanese, at the insistence of Germany, start strengthening the Kwantung Army of Manchuria to prepare for an invasion of the Soviet Union. While actual success would be limited, it is hoped that an offensive in the east would convince the Soviet Union to sue for peace. At the start of summer of 1945, the Japanese invaded the Soviet Union, catching the Soviets by surprise, as they believed that the Japanese would only have invaded in 1946, in the face of the massive American threat. The Soviets were defeated rapidly, and despite enormous supply difficulties, the Japanese were able to reach the outskirts of Vladivostok the winter of 1945, threatening to cut off Allied Lend-Lease supply. As the winter of 1945 approached, the Japanese dug in, ready to capture Vladivostok when the weather gets warmer the following year. When the Soviets sue for peace in early 1946, the Japanese gain a strip of land on the coast, reaching all the way to the important port city of Vladivostok, and are given a lease on Soviet oil. The attack, despite using up large amounts of land forces from China, had no negative effect on the campaigns in the Pacific.

Chapter 12: The Last Zombie

In August of 1945, American bombers based in Tinian departed, carrying one nuclear bomb each. As each bomber flew over their targets, a single anti-aircraft gun shot down one of the bombers, while a Japanese fighter, one of the oldest models, flown by a pilot still in training, rammed the American bomber miraculously without being shot down on his own initiative. Both bombs exploded spectacularly, but little material damage was done. Radiation, however, killed many people over Hiroshima and Nagasaki, creating many zombies which were ferried to the frontline. A massive shock hit the American government, which was hoping to use these new superweapons to end the war. The Japanese government, seeing the massive explosions the destruction of both American bombers caused, recognizes the American completion of a nuclear bomb, which the Japanese themselves have barely been able to start the construction of. Three more American nuclear weapons will be ready in September, and an equal amount in October. While the IJN recovers and waits for their new Unryu class carries to be ready, in spring of 1945, American troops land in the Philippines, and with the new tactic of keeping the chainsaw tanks in reserve until all regular forces are defeated, therefore making zombies a small threat, the Americans secure it by the end of 1945, despite fierce Japanese opposition. Although most Japanese attempts at destroying the six nuclear bombs in 1946 are beaten by strong American resistance, a single fighter was able to go through multilayered defenses, preventing an American attack on Tokyo from taking place. However, nuclear attacks on Kokura, a second attack on Hiroshima, Yokohama, Niigata, and a second attack on Nagasaki all succeed. Miraculously, despite being built in Nagasaki, the fleet carrier Amagi was at Kobe that day, and escaped being destroyed. The enormous casualties in these five attacks convince the Japanese, who have been trying to seek a peace treaty since 1942, that to gain a peace treaty without unconditional surrender, a final last stand must be made. This would be either at the home islands, where new units are being rapidly raised, or at

Formosa, where large amounts of Japanese transport ships are stationed, ready to ferry large amounts of Japanese troops from China to Formosa. After the conquest of the Philippines, the Americans have a strong base to intercept Japanese supply ships and combined with the atomic bomb attacks and regular bomb attacks increasing in intensity, the Japanese economy dwindles. Hoping to tie up and destroy large amounts of Japanese forces before the invasion of the home islands, coupled with lower casualties than expected in the Philippines campaign, Formosa is planned to be invaded, with American troops moving into the Amoy beachhead at the same time, the final invasion before the attack on the Japanese home islands. In the spring of 1946, American air strikes on Formosa alert the Japanese to a possible American invasion. Knowing that this is Japan's last chance to kill enough Americans so that a peace treaty will be achieved without unconditional surrender, the Japanese send almost all aircraft defending the home islands from China to Formosa, and as many men from Northern China, particularly as the end of the Soviet campaign allowed the Japanese to move forces from the Kwantung Army southwards, are rushed to Formosa, using the new tactic of heavily built fortifications manned by regular soldiers pinning down American forces, and zombies released to swarm the attacking Americans, before disappearing underground again, via a zombie mind control ray based on Germany's technology. All Japanese naval units, including the three new Unryu class carriers with their full air groups, are ordered to sortie for a final naval battle, with carrier forces totaling seven fleet carriers and two light carriers. With the loss of much of Japan's fuel supply following the fall of the Philippines, large amounts of fuel obtained from the Soviet Union were kept in reserve, which are now able to fuel the large amounts of naval units and aircraft involved in the Formosa campaign. However, a massive American fleet, consisting of fourteen battleships, including one battleship repaired from the massive naval battle with the Germans and transferred from the Atlantic, and eleven fleet carriers, each one larger than the Japanese carriers, oppose them. To counter the enormous amounts of

American carriers, large amounts of land-based aircraft are launched from Formosa, combined with a new Japanese tactic where if an aircraft is damaged beyond repair, the pilot would use the aircraft to ram an American ship in a final strike before the aircraft's destruction. With the enormous amounts of land-based aircraft, the Japanese forces outnumbers the American aircraft forces. With the support of strike submarines with the priority of sinking American carriers, Japanese aircraft launch a massive air raid on the American carriers and battleships, sinking both North Carolina class battleships and one fleet carrier, crippling one fleet carrier and one battleship, and damaging four more battleships and one fleet carrier, along with the destruction of large amounts of American aircraft and countless amounts of cruisers and destroyers sunk, crippled, and damaged. Enormous amounts of anti-aircraft fire, along with effective combat air patrol and changes in American tactics catching the Japanese by surprise, cause large amounts of casualties, although the Japanese still outnumber American aircraft forces. An American counterstrike, aimed at sinking the Japanese carriers, sink the aircraft carriers Chitose, Chyioda, and Hiyo, while crippling the Taiho. A second Japanese air strike, aided by submarines sinking the crippled American aircraft carrier Franklin and the damaged battleship West Virginia, sink the crippled battleship Iowa, the crippled aircraft carrier Randolph, and the damaged battleships Maryland and Tennessee, with the Japanese air forces taking more casualties. Two more strikes on both sides leave the Japanese fleet carriers Taiho, Junyo, and Unryu sunk, the Amagi and Katuragi crippled, and Zuikaku damaged. The American losses include the battleships Massachusetts, Pennsylvania, New Jersey, and Wisconsin sunk, the South Dakota crippled and the Alabama and Indiana damaged, and the American fleet carriers Boxer, Antietam, Lake Champlain, and Bennington sunk, the Bon Homme Richard and Hancock crippled, and Ticonderoga, Antietam, and Shangri-La damaged, and gigantic amounts of destroyers and cruisers sunk, crippled, and damaged. The aircraft forces on both sides are decimated, and the

Japanese carrier force withdraws, losing the Amagi to American submarine attacks in the process. However, the final Japanese submarine strikes of the war sinks the battleships Alabama and South Dakota, and in an enormous surprise success, a single salvo by the Japanese submarine I-19 sinks the crippled fleet carrier Hancock and the damaged battleship Indiana. The massive air and naval battle off Formosa leave the Japanese navy and air forces broken, in no position to intercept an American attack against the Japanese home islands. After several weeks of intense American bombardment, the first American troops land on the beaches of Formosa and Amoy. As the Japanese expected, a long campaign, lasting throughout 1946 and into early 1947 was hard fought on Formosa, killing so many Americans that the government started considering Japanese peace overtures, while on Amoy, a long American campaign pushing against the enormous Japanese army in China, in conjunction with a renewed Chinese offensive following unit transfers to Formosa in southern China succeeds, linking up with

American forces, moving northwards, reaching the outskirts of Shanghai by the end of 1946, and after a long, costly, street battle, Shanghai is liberated by American forces, while a larger Chinese offensive past Shanghai push the Japanese back to Manchuria. With more and more American resources diverted from the planned invasion of the Japanese home islands involved in China by 1947, the end of the European war allows the transfer of large amounts of the army to the Pacific, and with reinforcements, American forces in China, together with Chinese forces, coordinate a combined assault, pushing the Japanese out of China, beginning an invasion of Korea. The large Kwantung Army resists fiercely causing so many American casualties, that, along with the costly Formosa campaign and the enormous amounts of zombies created and the massive associated extermination operations, convinces the Americans to make peace with Japan in the summer of 1947, when Seoul was liberated. The peace treaty's terms stipulate that Japan would give up all Chinese holdings, including Hainan and Formosa, Korea, and the

Philippines. However, the Japanese will keep all holdings in southeast Asia, including French Indochina, Thailand, and Malaysia, with Burma serving as a buffer zone between the British in India and the Japanese. Japan also controls the Dutch East Indies and the territories annexed at the end of World War 1, although the loss of both the Philippines and Formosa worry the Japanese about the security of sea lanes. Acknowledging this, the Allies pledge to not station major naval units in the independent Philippines or at Formosa. No economic reparations of any kind are required, and the current Japanese government, army, and navy are allowed to survive and continue. With the signing of the peace treaty aboard the American battleship Missouri, ending the war in the Pacific, World War 2, the most destructive war, ends. With large amounts of American forces already in China, and with a slightly antagonistic Japan, the American armies stationed in a fully democratic Korea and in China intervene in the Chinese Civil War, to prevent China from falling to communism and gaining an important ally in Asia. After huge amounts of attrition, the Chinese communist army finally falls, and encircled in Manchuria while attempting to escape to the Soviet border, Mao Zedong, not wishing to be captured like Tito, commits suicide in 1951. The resulting defeat of communists in both China and Yugoslavia create enormous amounts of zombies, which a joint UN force, of Japanese, German, American, Soviet, French, Chinese, and British forces, along with many other units joining in from other countries, work together to eradicate the zombie threat from Normandy and Britain to Korea and Guadalcanal. This massive effort of teamwork between the recently warring nations of World War 2 helps stabilize post war relations. In 1949, exactly on the twentieth anniversary of the invasion of Poland, starting World War 2, Adolf Hitler dies, at 60 years old. Following the death of the Fuhrer, Hitler's successor Herman Goering dissolves the Nazi state, repeals all antisemitic laws, and transforms Germany into a democratic constitutional monarchy, with him as chancellor, which despite not having much power, grants him much fame and public appearance. Prince

Wilhelm Of Prussia, grandchild of the last German Kaiser, who survived his service in the Battle Of France, becomes the first German Kaiser of this new government. By 1960, the last single zombie holdout, hiding underground in Smolensk, was hunted down, and destroyed by a single British soldier in a Z.I.B.R.A suit and ironically, supported by one Soviet and German soldier. Meanwhile, as Japan rebuilds after the war, supported by the US, hoping to rebuild what was destroyed by nuclear weapons, relations between Japan and the Americans greatly smooth, with Japan eventually become a powerful superpower and a close American ally. With China allied with the Americans and crippled by the loss of some of the most important western territories, a weak Soviet Union is far outproduced by the US, becoming a small threat, allowing the US to be the world's most powerful superpower, fighting across the newly decolonized Africa and the Middle East to convert those areas into American allies, with much success. After the collapse of the Soviet Union in 1971, a new, friendlier, Russia, Kazakhstan, and many new countries, all adopt democracy and become American allies. By 1980, through a series of agreements and mediated peace treaties by the UN, led by the US, world peace is achieved.

Printed in Great Britain
by Amazon